It's a Perfect Day

Abigail Pizer

J. B. Lippincott New York

It's A Perfect Day
Copyright © 1990 by Abigail Pizer
First published by Macmillan Children's Books, London.
All rights reserved. No part of this book may be
used or reproduced in any manner whatsoever without
written permission except in the case of brief quotations
embodied in critical articles and reviews. Printed in Belgium.
For information address
J. B. Lippincott Junior Books, 10 East 53rd Street,
New York, N.Y. 10022.

Library of Congress Cataloging-in-Publication Data is available:
LC Card Number 89-37937

1 2 3 4 5 6 7 8 9 10
First American Edition

As the sun rises over the hill. . .

the birds start to sing and the animals
begin to wake up.

It's a perfect day to crow,
thought the rooster.

Cock-a-doodle-doo!

The says, Cock-a-doodle-doo!

What a perfect day!

It's a perfect day to collect some pollen,
thought the bee.

Buzz buzz!

The  says, Cock-a-doodle-doo!

The says, Buzz buzz!

What a perfect day!

It's a perfect day to have a nap,
thought the cat.

Purr purr!

The  says, Cock-a-doodle-doo!

The says, Buzz buzz!

The says, Purr purr!

What a perfect day!

It's a perfect day to eat some buttercups, thought the cow.

Moo moo!

The  says, Cock-a-doodle-doo!

The says, Buzz buzz!

The says, Purr purr!

The  says, Moo moo!

What a perfect day!

It's a perfect day to swim in the pond,
thought the duck.

Quack quack!

The  says, Cock-a-doodle-doo!

The says, Buzz buzz!

The says, Purr purr!

The says, Moo moo!

The says, Quack quack!

What a perfect day!

It's a perfect day to wallow in the mud, thought the pig.

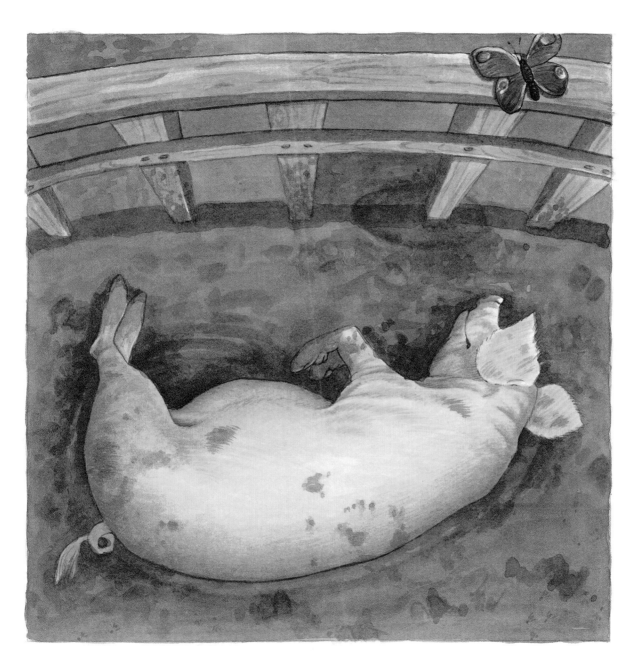

Oink oink!

The  says, Cock-a-doodle-doo!

The says, Buzz buzz!

The says, Purr purr!

The says, Moo moo!

The says, Quack quack!

The  says, Oink oink!

What a perfect day!

It's a perfect day to eat some corn,
thought the mouse.

Squeak squeak!

The  says, Cock-a-doodle-doo!

The says, Buzz buzz!

The says, Purr purr!

The  says, Moo moo!

The says, Quack quack!

The  says, Oink oink!

The says, Squeak squeak!

What a perfect day!

It's a perfect day to chase the cat,
thought the goose.

Honk honk!

The  says, Cock-a-doodle-doo!

The says, Buzz buzz!

The says, Purr purr!

The  says, Moo moo!

The says, Quack quack!

The  says, Oink oink!

The says, Squeak squeak!

The says, Honk honk!

What a perfect day!

It's a perfect day to bark at the ducks,
thought the dog.

Woof woof!

The  says, Cock-a-doodle-doo!

The says, Buzz buzz!

The says, Purr purr!

The  says, Moo moo!

The says, Quack quack!

The says, Oink oink!

The says, Squeak squeak!

The says, Honk honk!

The says, Woof woof!

What a perfect day!

It's a perfect day to gallop around the field,
thought the horse.

Neigh neigh!

What a perfect day!